Nyla's
New Shoes

Written by
Caitlin Nickel
Illustrated by
Vivien Sarkany

For everyone who has ever experienced change and had eyes to see the possibilities that came with it!

Nyla LOVED her new purple suede shoes!

She hadn't had a brand-new pair of shoes in a long time.

She usually wore her cousin's brown, hand-me-down shoes, or wore no shoes at all.

She didn't mind wearing hand-me-downs, and she didn't mind going barefoot, but this was something special.

They were soft.

They were purple.

They were perfect.

Most importantly, they were hers!

The shoes were a little stiff at first.

Even though she walked carefully, so she wouldn't get them filthy, they still managed to bring up a few unwelcome blisters.

This never happened with hand-me-down shoes.

Nyla didn't care.

She wore them while she ate.

She wore them to school.

She wore them to the park.

She wore them to swimming lessons, and almost jumped right into the pool with the shoes STILL on her feet!

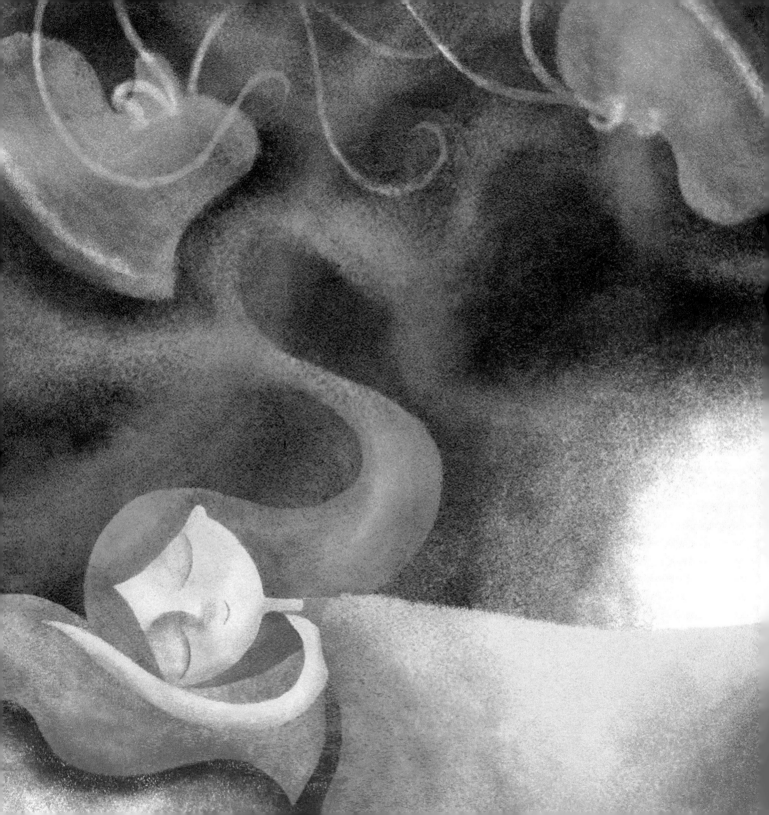

Nyla even tried to wear her shoes to bed!

Her parents lovingly removed them from her feet each night, but couldn't remove them from her dreams.

Before long, the blisters went away
and the stiff new-ness of the shoes
disappeared entirely.

Nyla had so many wonderful adventures in those shoes!
She seemed to dance everywhere she went.

She would pretend they were magic shoes that left flowers
springing up in the footsteps she left behind.

Months went by while Nyla lived her life in those shoes. Then the shoes began to show signs of wear.

The left shoe had a small stain where Nyla had spilled milk on it during breakfast.

A small hole in the heel of the right shoe began to appear, but Nyla's Mother easily patched it with a scrap of old jeans.

Eventually, the day came when something happened to Nyla's purple shoes that couldn't be patched or cleaned.

Nyla tried to put her shoes on one morning... and her foot didn't fit!

Oh no!

She raced to find her mother, hoping
with every bit of her heart that her mother
could fix it.

She couldn't.

Nyla watched, brokenheartedly, as her mother left her purple suede shoes at the donation center that afternoon.

Her mother said that the purple shoes would go on to make another little girl's life more magical.

But what about Nyla?

Later that evening, Nyla's parents pulled out a new pretty package, with a new pair of shoes inside.

Nyla opened it and saw...

...a pair of green flats.

She was sad. She thanked her parents for the new shoes and then went barefoot to bed.

The next day, she decided to at least TRY the green flats.

They were squishy on the bottom of her foot, and she liked that, but they rubbed on the top of her toes, and she DIDN'T like that.

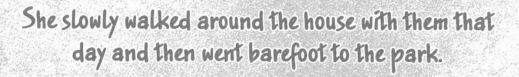

She slowly walked around the house with them that day and then went barefoot to the park.

The next day, she tried them again.

She wore them as far as the mailbox at the end of her driveway, but she went barefoot to swimming lessons.

The next day, Nyla wore her green flats to the park to play with her friends.

She took them off when she chased frogs by the park pond.

She kept them off while she and her friends hung upside down on the monkey bars and made silly monkey sounds.

The flats stayed off when Nyla rolled down the big park hill, racing her friends to the bottom.

When everyone finally stopped to catch their breath,
something caught Nyla's eye.

Sitting on a park bench nearby, was a girl a little younger than Nyla. She sat shyly with her parents, watching the other children play.

What caught Nyla's attention were the shoes the girl was wearing.

She recognized the small milk stain on the left shoe.

Nyla's heart seemed to skip a beat as she looked at those shoes.

She thought of all the memories they held.

What adventures had they been on without her?

She looked up from the shoes, to the girl's shy face.

That girl looked like she could use some magic in her life

Nyla put on her green flats and walked over to the girl wearing her old purple shoes.

Do you want to play with us?

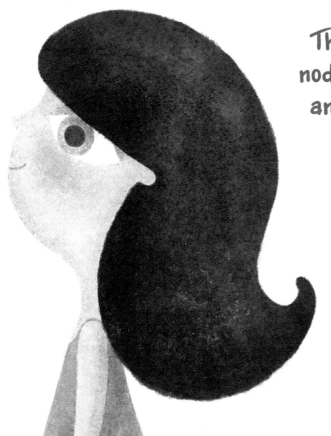

The girl looked at her parents, who nodded approvingly, then smiled wide and took Nyla's outstretched hand.

Nyla led her **new friend** over to her old friends and
they sat down on the grass together. She looked at
their feet, side by side; the wonderful **purple** shoes,
and the green flats.

Perhaps these flats held some adventure in them
after all.

She looked over her shoulder where their feet had
trampled the grass. There, in the middle of their
footprints, two flowers began to bloom.

A portion of proceeds from each sale of "Nyla's New Shoes" is donated to Hogar Sapucay in Argentina.

Hogar Sapucay (Sapucay Children's Center), is a day-home for children at risk located in Northern Argentina. It is a Christian nonprofit organization that serves over 90 children by providing nutritious meals, help with homework, bible studies, extracurricular activities, and the love and support these children desperately long for. The center's goal is that each child would come to know Jesus personally, be shown how cherished and loved they are and to stop the cycle of violence and abuse so prevalent in the area.

Thank YOU for choosing this book and for helping this essential ministry in Argentina!

CPSIA information can be obtained
at www.ICGtesting.com
Printed in the USA
BVHW020229120622
639533BV00003B/75

9 781777 370138